We All Hs

by Maryellen Gregoire

Consultant:
Adria F. Klein, Ph.D.
California State University, San Bernardino

capstone
classroom

Heinemann Raintree • Red Brick Learning
division of Capstone

The sun shines light on us.

Lamps shine light on us.

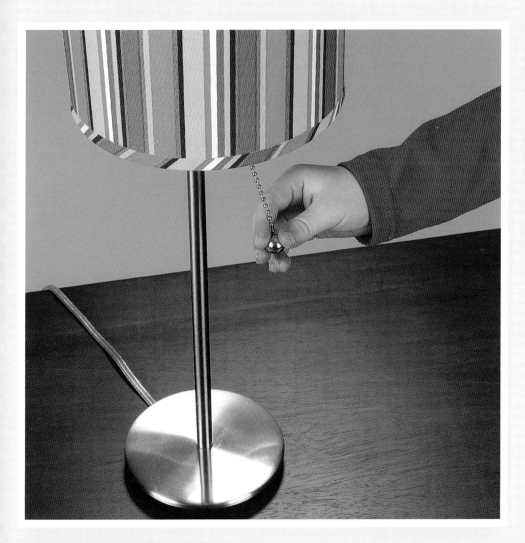

Candles shine light on us.

Light shines on us in many ways.

Light shines through windows.

Light shines through colored glass.

When light cannot shine through something, it makes a shadow.

When the sun is shining, everything has a shadow.

Light cannot go through this girl. She has a shadow.

Light cannot go through this boy. He has a shadow.

Sometimes a shadow
is big.

Sometimes a shadow is small.

Shadows can jump with you.

Shadows can run with you.

Can you hide your shadow?